ICOSA

FLY
AWAY
HOME By JACK KENT

DAVID McKAY COMPANY, INC.

Copyright © 1969 by Jack Kent
All Rights Reserved
Manufactured in the United States of America

Library of Congress Catalog Card No. 69-13436

Fly Away Home

To June and Junior,
who make *my* house "home"

At half past two on a warm Tuesday afternoon in May was just the right time to be doing nothing in particular, and Sally was doing it in the garden by the red rose bush.

As she bent over to sniff
a rose, she noticed a ladybug
on one of the leaves.

Everybody has to have a name so you can call them by it, and Sally decided that the ladybug's name was Mrs. Mildred.

"Good afternoon, Mrs. Mildred," said Sally.

The ladybug was out of breath from climbing up the rose bush and merely nodded in reply.

"Aren't the roses beautiful?" Sally asked.

Mrs. Mildred didn't answer.

"A conversation isn't a conversation if only one person is doing it," said Sally. "It's more like a *recitation*."

Mrs. Mildred still didn't say anything. So Sally stood up straight, folded her hands in front of her, cleared her throat, and began to recite:

"Ladybug,
ladybug,
Fly away
home.
Your house
is on fire,
Your children
will burn."

Noticing that Mrs. Mildred seemed quite upset, Sally cried, "Oh, I beg your pardon! Your house isn't *really* on fire," Sally explained. "It's just a nursery rhyme. I'm sorry if I worried you."

But Mrs. Mildred still seemed upset, and Sally was sure she saw tears in her eyes.

"I'll bet I know what's the matter," said Sally. "You don't *have* a home! That's it, isn't it?"

Mrs. Mildred didn't deny it.

"Well, you come with me and we'll *find* you a home," said Sally.

"Birds live in nests," said
Sally. "Would you like a nest
for a home?"

Mrs. Mildred
wouldn't.

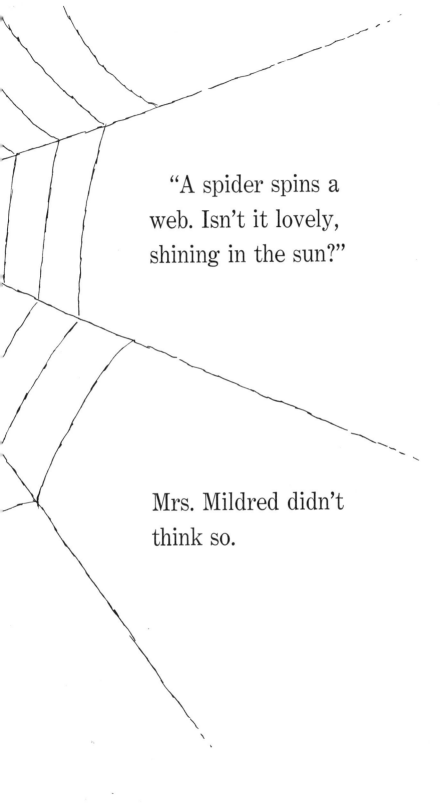

"A spider spins a web. Isn't it lovely, shining in the sun?"

Mrs. Mildred didn't think so.

"Bees live in a hive and make honey," said Sally. "There's a beehive in this hollow tree."

Mrs. Mildred wasn't interested.

"Ants live in ant hills.

They're full of tunnels and
secret passages."
    Mrs. Mildred looked bored.

"Dogs live in kennels.

But *ours* likes my *bed* better."

Sally laughed.
Mrs. Mildred didn't.

"Bears live in caves and hibernate all winter. They even sleep right through mealtimes."

Mrs. Mildred was dozing.

Sally woke her up to show
her the hole in the garage wall
—the one that Daddy kept
meaning to cover up, but hadn't
got around to yet.

"A mouse
lives in
there,"
said
Sally.

"Moles live in holes, too.

Don't you like any of these homes, Mrs. Mildred?"

Without answering, Mrs. Mildred flew out of Sally's hand,
lit on the ground, and crawled
under a rock.

"Well, I suppose that sort of a home will *do*," Sally said, "for a *bug*. But what *I* think is the very best sort of a home," said Sally...

"is a house," she said,

"like mine!"